S0-FAF-420

This book belongs to:

_____

Copyright 2024
Ann Eckhart / Bowker

ISBN: 978-1-956047-57-8

Cover Design by Ann Eckhart

Where Did Papa Go?

by Ann Eckhart

Dedicated to our loving Papa,
who we miss every day.

Charlie & Teddy

Charlie and Teddy are two pugs so sweet,
They love to run and play and especially eat.

With toys scattered around, they romp, and they play,
Happy and active all through the day.

Outside in the grass under the sky so blue,
They sometimes chased balls that their Mommy threw.

Whether snowy winters or rainy springs, it's true,
Through autumn's falling leaves, there was so much to do.

And when they would tire, they'd happily lay,
Basking in the sun after they played.

But as nighttime came and shadows grew long,
They'd seek out a snuggle where they belonged.

Since they were puppies, one lap was always there,
Papa, their grandpa, had much love to spare.

On a cozy couch, under blankets so plush,
Papa's lap was a haven, a comforting hush.

As the boys grew up, their naps were more sweet,
In the warmth of Papa's lap, their favorite seat.

Under the TV's warm glow, they snored in their sleep,
But when Mommy called 'Dinner!', they lept up from their heap.

But then came a time, so sudden and sad,
When Papa stayed in bed, which made them feel bad.

"Boys, stay down," their Mommy would say,
I'm sorry, but you can't sit on Papa's lap today."

Charlie and Teddy, with their brown eyes so wide,
Looked on as their Mommy stayed close to Papa's side.

"Boys," Mommy whispered to them, "didn't you know?
Papa is my Daddy, loved more than I can show.

I promised to care for him each and every day,
Just like I care for you in every single way."

Charlie and Teddy listened quiet and still,
As Mommy told a story that gave them a chill.

"My own Mommy went to heaven quite early, you see,
Papa raised me alone, and we were as close as can be.

He juggled work and my care with love and with grace,
Meeting my needs and my wants in every time and place.

So, I made a promise to take care of him,
When came the time his life started to dim.

Now that time has come, and Papa needs me,
I have to be strong to help him be free."

Charlie and Teddy watched on in fear,
Knowing that something dreadful was near.

The house filled with people, both familiar and new,
Nurses and aides seemed to know what to do.

Uncles and aunts and grandchildren came,
Each of them whispering their sweet Papa's name.

Mommy was sad and had tears in her eyes,
And a new word was heard about when someone dies.

Charlie and Teddy snuggled together with care,
There were no laps available, just Papa's empty chair.

Then, one morning, Papa's bed was bare,
His body was gone, yet the dogs sensed his care.

Mommy sat down with a new story to tell,
About a place where loved pets and their owners went to dwell.

"Before you boys, " Mommy said with a smile,
"there were two more,
Max and Lucy, two cute pugs like you, whom Papa adored.

Max and Lucy loved to play in the sun,
Just like you two, they loved to have fun.

They, too, napped on Papa's lap, just like you boys,
They loved Papa so much, and they brought him much joy."

"But as Max and Lucy aged, they grew slow and weak,
Finding comfort and peace was what I, their Mommy, did seek.

Max and Lucy, our beloved pets from before,
journeyed to the Rainbow Bridge through a very special door.

At this bridge, pets wait, their hearts full of love,
For the day their owners join them to the world above.

Years may pass on Earth, a long, winding road,
But for pets, it's just a moment, in their heavenly abode.

And when that day comes, we'll all walk through that door,
And be greeted by loved ones who we knew from before."

"Papa is now there," Mommy said with a smile,
"He will await us there, too, but not for a long while.

In the meantime, Max and Lucy will hold Papa tight,
Hugging and assuring him that everything is alright.

And Papa is happy in a land without pain,
Bathed in warmth and love until we see him again."

Mommy, Charlie and Teddy miss Papa, it's true,
But they remember the love and the good times, too.

They think of the cuddles, giggles, and fun,
The naps in the sun, and the grass where they'd run.

And though Papa was gone, in their hearts, he stayed near,
In every memory, they knew Papa was still here.

So Charlie and Teddy, with hearts brave and strong,
Learned that loving someone means they're never gone.

They now keep Papa's love in each game that they play,
In the cuddles at night and the naps through the day.

They remember his favorites, his jokes and his snacks,
They laugh, recalling his fun, playful acts.

And when they get sleepy, as dogs often do,
They dream of the Rainbow Bridge, bright and true.

Through the special door to another land, so bright,
Charlie and Teddy know they'll step into the light.

A place of joy where all is right and true,
Together with Papa, in a world anew.

With each wag of their tails, each playful bark,
Charlie and Teddy honor Papa, a light in the dark.

For love never leaves; it just changes its form,
In memories, in dreams, in the calm after the storm.

Papa's lap may be gone, but Mommy is still here,
And she needs their love and holds them so dear.

People on Earth need cuddles and love,
As those who've gone before them look on from above.

So, to all little pugs and children alike,
Remember, love lasts, like a star shining bright.

Even when we can't see those who are gone,
In our hearts and our dreams, their love lives on.

Hi, friends! Thank you for reading our first book. We have more adventures to share. Go to our Mommy's website at AnnEckhart.com so you don't miss out on any of our stories!
Love, Charlie & Teddy